Vernon Grant's
Santa Claus

Accompanying texts by Mary Lynn Norton

HARRY N. ABRAMS, INC., PUBLISHERS

IN ASSOCIATION WITH

THE YORK COUNTY

CULTURE & HERITAGE COMMISSION

Breakfast with Santa, 1971

Contents

The Night Before Christmas, circa 1968

Introduction

Renowned creator of *Snap!® Crackle!® Pop!®*, illustrator Vernon Grant built his reputation on his signature gnomes and a whimsical approach to illustration. But more than any other subject, Grant enjoyed drawing Santa Claus. Every summer for much of his career, Grant's studio was transformed into a Christmas wonderland as he worked to meet the July deadline for magazines and commercial accounts with holiday offerings. From this annual ritual came the tradition of creating a special Santa card for his family and friends. Santa soon became his favorite character, and Grant spoke of him as an old friend. "Many people ask me what Santa and I talk about," he said. "But Santa doesn't talk to me at all. He doesn't mind if I look in on him from time to time, however. We have a pretty good relationship."

Vernon Grant drew his very first Santa Claus around the age of seven. His teacher gave the class a picture of Santa Claus and told the students to trace or copy the picture. But Vernon had bigger ideas. He experimented with his drawing until he concluded that he could portray Santa better than the artist in the magazine. From that day on, he never tired of developing his own ways to draw the jolly old fellow and depict the magic of the holiday season.

Grant's first published Santa appeared on the cover of the December issue of *Ladies' Home Journal* in 1932. Over the next half century, more than a hundred of his holiday illustrations would be published as Christmas cards, advertisements, and magazine covers. Grant was never at a loss for drawing a different Santa each year, often employing his signature black background to enhance Santa's commanding presence. One portrait even has Santa in a snow-white suit with blue trim. Chuckling quietly, Grant once explained, "Santa is a lot like most of us. He likes a change, too." Throughout his career, Grant took the liberty of depicting Santa in very real and timely situations, from a penniless Santa during the Great Depression to a Santa who reminds busy shoppers, "Don't forget the true gifts of the holiday season!" Vernon Grant's illustrative magic always delivered a memorable Santa Claus for the young and the young at heart.

Mary Lynn Norton
CURATOR OF ART
YORK COUNTY CULTURE & HERITAGE COMMISSION

Classy Santa, circa 1960s

Santa's Christmas Wish, 1970

We Wish You a Merry Christmas

We wish you a Merry Christmas,
We wish you a Merry Christmas,
We wish you a Merry Christmas,
And a Happy New Year.

Good tidings to you,
And all of your kin,
Good tidings for Christmas,
And a Happy New Year.

We all know that Santa's coming,
We all know that Santa's coming,
We all know that Santa's coming,
And soon will be here.

Good tidings to you,
And all of your kin,
Good tidings for Christmas,
And a Happy New Year.

We wish you a Merry Christmas,
We wish you a Merry Christmas,
We wish you a Merry Christmas,
And a Happy New Year.

Kittie to Santa Claus

Jolly old Kriss, what a fellow you are
Riding all over the world in the air,
Sliding down chimneys through ashes and smoke,
Fur-covered Kriss, you're a regular joke.

How do you manage to carry such loads?
How do you manage to keep the right roads?
How do you know all the good girls and boys?
Why don't we wake with your clatter and noise?

How can you guess what we all like best?
How can you please all the birds in the nest?
What are you doing the rest of the year?
Sleeping, I s'pose, with your little reindeer.

If I thought you'd appear with a shout and a caper,
Jolly and fat like the one in the paper,
I'd keep awake; but I know that you stay,
When children are watching, quite out of the way.

Nick & Gnome Share Secrets, 1953

Christmas Greetings, 1942

A Christmas Tree

BY CHARLES DICKENS

Household Words (December 21, 1850)

I have been looking at a merry company of children assembled round that pretty German toy, a Christmas Tree. The tree was planted in the middle of a great round table, and towered high above their heads. It was brilliantly lighted by a multitude of little tapers; and everywhere sparkled and glittered with bright objects. There were rosy-cheeked dolls, hiding behind the green leaves; and there were real watches (with movable hands, at least, and an endless capacity of being wound up) dangling from innumerable twigs; there were French-polished tables, chairs, bedsteads, wardrobes, eight-day clocks, and various other articles of domestic furniture (wonderfully made in tin), perched among the boughs, as if in preparation for some fairy housekeeping; there were jolly, broad-faced little men, much more agreeable in appearance than many real men—and no wonder, for their heads took off, and showed them to be full of sugar-plums; there were trinkets for the elder girls, far brighter than any grown-up gold and jewels; there were baskets and pincushions in all devices; there were guns, swords, and banners; there were witches standing in enchanted rings of pasteboard, to tell fortunes; there were teetotums, humming-tops, needle-cases, pen-wipers, smelling-bottles, conversation-cards, bouquet-holders; real fruit, made artificially dazzling with gold leaf; imitation apples, pears, and walnuts, crammed with surprises; in short, as a pretty child, before me, delightedly whispered to another pretty child, her bosom friend, "There was everything, and more."

A Letter to Santa Claus

BY ANNA D. WALKER (c. 1890)

I've written a letter to Santa Claus;
    Would you like to know the reason?
'Tis very plain and just because
    We've moved this present season.
I'm always called a happy child,
    Yet for weeks I've had this worry—
Will Santa Claus know that we're here,
    Or pass us in his hurry?

I told him not to pass us by,
    And gave our street and number—
He cannot tell by faces; why?
    He comes while we all slumber;
Besides, I've had some other fears—
    Our chimney is so narrow
It will not hold old Santa's wares,
    It scarce would hold a barrow.

I've given him quite a list of things;
    Of dolls and little dishes,
Of skates and sleds, and kites and strings,
    And many other wishes;
I said, "Dear Santa, please do come,
    Nor mind the narrow passage,
For every child within the home
    Has sent to you this message."

Santa's Special Delivery, 1940

Hi–Ho! For a Merry Christmas, 1932

Returning Home with the Spoils

Anonymous poem in *Harper's Bazaar* (January 6, 1877)

Oh! we've all been shopping, shop, shop, shopping,
    We've bought our Christmas gifts, and had a tiresome promenade;
And we're all of us a-dropping, drop, drop, dropping
    Fast asleep, except papa, that idle man, who only paid.

When we were busy choosing, choose, choose, choosing,
    He merely yawned at intervals behind his *porte-monnaie;*
So now while we are losing, lose, lose, losing
    Ourselves in dreams, he's wide awake—he only had to pay.

From
Yes, Virginia, There Is a Santa Claus

BY FRANCIS P. CHURCH

Editorial Page, *New York Sun*, 1897

We take pleasure in answering thus prominently the communication below, expressing at the same time our great gratification that its faithful author is numbered among the friends of *The Sun*:

> Dear Editor,
> I am 8 years old. Some of my little friends say there is no Santa Claus. Papa says, "If you see it in *The Sun*, it's so." Please tell me the truth, is there a Santa Claus?
>
> *Virginia O'Hanlon*

Virginia, your little friends are wrong. They have been affected by the skepticism of a skeptical age. They do not believe except what they see. They think that nothing can be which is not comprehensible by their little minds. All minds, Virginia, whether they be men's or children's, are little. In this great universe of ours, man is a mere insect, an ant, in his intellect as compared with the boundless world about him, as measured by the intelligence capable of grasping the whole of truth and knowledge.

Yes, Virginia, there is a Santa Claus. He exists as certainly as love and generosity and devotion exist, and you know that they abound and give to your life its highest beauty and joy. Alas! how dreary would be the world if there were no Santa Claus! It would be as dreary as if there were no Virginias. There would be no childlike faith then, no poetry, no romance to make tolerable this existence. We should have no enjoyment, except in sense and sight. The external light with which childhood fills the world would be extinguished.

I Got Your Letter…, 1934

Spiffy Claus, 1956

A December Ditty

BY ALICE WILLIAMS BROTHERTON

St. Nicholas (January 1891)

The Holly, oh, the Holly!
    Green leaf, and berry red,
Is the plant that thrives in winter
    "When all the rest are fled."
When snows are on the ground,
    And the skies are gray and drear,
The Holly comes at Christmas-tide
    And brings the Christmas cheer.
Sing the Mistletoe, the Ivy,
    And the Holly-bush so gay,
That come to us in winter—
    No summer friends are they.

Give me the sturdy friendship
    That will ever loyal hold,
And give me the hardy Holly
    That dares the winter's cold;
Oh, the roses bloom in June,
    When the skies are bright and clear,
But the Holly comes at Christmas-tide
    The best time o' the year.
Sing the Holly, and the Ivy,
    And the merry Mistletoe,
That come to us in winter
    When the fields are white with snow!

Beggar's Rhyme

Christmas is coming, the geese are getting fat,
Please to put a penny in the old man's hat;
If you haven't got a penny, a ha'penny will do,
If you haven't got a ha'penny, God bless you.

Empty Pockets, 1936

Don't Forget!, 1952

If You're Good

BY JAMES COURTNEY CHALLISS

St. Nicholas (December 1896)

Santa Claus'll come to-night,
    If you're *good*,
And do what you know is right,
    As you should;
Down the chimney he will creep,
Bringing you a wooly sheep,
And a doll that goes to sleep;—
    If you're *good*.

Santa Claus will drive his sleigh
    Thro' the wood,
But he'll come around this way
    If you're *good*,
With a wind-up bird that sings,
And a puzzle made of rings—
Jumping-jacks and funny things—
    If you're *good*.

Santa grieves when you are bad,
    As he should;
But it makes him very glad
    When you're *good*.
He is wise, and he's a dear;
Just do right and never fear;
He'll remember you each year,
    If you're *good*.

From

A Kidnapped Santa Claus

BY L. FRANK BAUM

Santa Claus lives in the Laughing Valley, where stands the big, rambling castle in which his toys are manufactured. His workmen, selected from the ryls, knooks, pixies and fairies, live with him, and every one is as busy as can be from one year's end to another.

Santa's Seal of Approval, 1976

Santa's Snappy Shine, 1978

Shoe or Stocking?

BY EDITH M. THOMAS

In Holland, children set their shoes,
  This night, outside the door;
These wooden shoes Knecht Clobes sees,
  And fills them from his store.

But here we hang our stockings up
  On handy hook or nail;
And Santa Claus, when all is still,
  Will plump them, without fail.

Speak out, you "Sober-sides," speak out,
  And let us hear your views;
Between a stocking and a shoe,
  What do you see to choose?

One instant pauses Sober-sides,
  A little sigh to fetch—
"Well, seems to me a stocking's best,
  For wooden shoes won't stretch!"

From

Santa Claus

BY FRED EMERSON BROOKS

I am that mythical, mystical thing—
The little ones' monarch, the children's king!
The mightiest ruler on earth am I,
My subjects outnumber the stars in the sky.
I'm ruler by right of the children's leave,
And visit them all on a Christmas Eve.

Santa's Stunning Reflection, 1973

Merrie Minstrels, 1937

From

Christmas

BY WILLIAM WORDSWORTH

The minstrels played their Christmas tune
 To-night beneath my cottage-eaves;
While smitten by a lofty moon,
 The encircling laurels thick with leaves
Gave back a rich and dazzling sheen,
That overpowered their natural green.

Through hill and valley every breeze
 Had sunk to rest with folded wings:
Keen was the air, but could not freeze
 Nor check the music of the strings;
So stout and hardy were the band
That scraped the cords with strenuous hand.

And who but listened?—till was paid
 Respect to every inmate's claim,
The greeting given, the music played
 In honor of each household name,
Duly pronounced with lusty call,
And a merry Christmas wished to all.

From

Around the World with Santa Claus

(adapted)

A Geographical Recreation

Come if you wish to join us; jump quickly in the sleigh;
Our reindeer team is ready, and we'll soon be underway.
Around the world with Santa Claus we're going to take our flight,
At speed that beats Miss Nellie Bly completely out of sight.

The World's Most Famous Traveler, 1972

Santa's Flying Golf Cart, 1980

From

Christmas News from the North

BY EDWIN L. SABIN

Automobiles in Lapland! Alas, then the end is near!
Good-by to the old-time Santa, his cutter and prancing deer;
Good-by to the blithesome jingle over the sleeping roofs;
Good-by to the welcome clatter of horns and eager hoofs;
Good-by to Donder and Blitzen and comrades fleet, good-by—
They yield to the brake and lever and thumbscrews X and Y!
Cometh the Christmas presents brought in a patent way;
Cometh the modern Santa, guiding his motor-sleigh!

Santa Claus Is Coming to Town

BY HAVEN GILLESPIE AND J. FRED COOTS

Oh! You better watch out,
You better not cry,
You better not pout,
I'm telling you why:
Santa Claus is coming to town!

He's making a list,
Checking it twice,
Gonna find out who's naughty or nice.
Santa Claus is coming to town!

He sees you when you're sleeping,
He knows when you're awake.
He knows if you've been bad or good,
So be good for goodness' sake!

Oh! You better watch out,
You better not cry,
You better not pout,
I'm telling you why:
Santa Claus is coming to town!

Santa Checking It Twice, II, circa 1977

Untitled, 1946

A Visit from St. Nicholas

BY CLEMENT CLARKE MOORE

'Twas the night before Christmas, when all through the house,
Not a creature was stirring, not even a mouse;
The stockings were hung by the chimney with care,
In hopes that ST. NICHOLAS soon would be there;
The children were nestled all snug in their beds,
While visions of sugar-plums danced in their heads;
And mamma in her 'kerchief, and I in my cap,
Had just settled down for a long winter's nap,
When out on the lawn there arose such a clatter,
I sprang from the bed to see what was the matter.
Away to the window I flew like a flash,
Tore open the shutters and threw up the sash.
The moon on the breast of the new-fallen snow
Gave the lustre of mid-day to objects below,
When, what to my wondering eyes should appear,
But a miniature sleigh, and eight tiny reindeer,
With a little old driver, so lively and quick,
I knew in a moment it must be St. Nick.

More rapid than eagles his coursers they came,
And he whistled, and shouted, and called them by name;
"Now, DASHER! now, DANCER! now, PRANCER and VIXEN!
On, COMET! on CUPID! on, DONDER and BLITZEN!
To the top of the porch! to the top of the wall!
Now dash away! dash away! dash away all!"
As dry leaves that before the wild hurricane fly,

When they meet with an obstacle, mount to the sky,
So up to the house-top the coursers they flew,
With the sleigh full of toys, and St. Nicholas too.
And then, in a twinkling, I heard on the roof
The prancing and pawing of each little hoof.
As I drew in my hand, and was turning around,
Down the chimney St. Nicholas came with a bound.
He was dressed all in fur, from his head to his foot,
And his clothes were all tarnished with ashes and soot;
A bundle of toys he had flung on his back,
And he looked like a peddler just opening his pack.
His eyes—how they twinkled! his dimples how merry!
His cheeks were like roses, his nose like a cherry!
His droll little mouth was drawn up like a bow,
And the beard of his chin was as white as the snow;
The stump of a pipe he held tight in his teeth,
And the smoke it encircled his head like a wreath;
He had a broad face and a little round belly,
That shook when he laughed like a bowl full of jelly.
He was chubby and plump, a right jolly old elf,
And I laughed when I saw him, in spite of myself;
A wink of his eye and a twist of his head,
Soon gave me to know I had nothing to dread;
He spoke not a word, but went straight to his work,
And filled all the stockings; then turned with a jerk,
And laying his finger aside of his nose,
And giving a nod, up the chimney he rose;
He sprang to his sleigh, to his team gave a whistle,
And away they all flew like the down of a thistle.
But I heard him exclaim, ere he drove out of sight,
"HAPPY CHRISTMAS TO ALL, AND TO ALL A GOOD-NIGHT."

A High Five From Santa, 1951

Santa Remembers Everyone, 1979

Kriss Kringle

BY THOMAS BAILEY ALDRICH

Just as the moon was fading
    Amid her misty rings,
And every stocking was stuffed
    With childhood's precious things,
Old Kriss Kringle looked round,
    And saw on the elm-tree bough,
High-hung, an oriole's nest,
    Silent and empty now.

"Quite like a stocking," he laughed,
    "Pinned up there on the tree!
Little I thought the birds
    Expected a present from me!"
Then old Kriss Kringle, who loves
    A joke as well as the best,
Dropped a handful of flakes
    In the oriole's empty nest.

From

Christmas Stories

CHARLES DICKENS

And I do come home at Christmas. We all do, or we all should. We all come home, or ought to come home, for a short holiday—the longer, the better—from the great boarding-school, where we are for ever working at our arithmetical slates, to take, and give a rest.

A Job Well Done, 1975

Santa's Band, 1974

Now Christmas Is Come

Now Christmas is come,
　　Let us beat up the drum,
And call all our neighbours together,
　　And when they appear,
　　Let us make them good cheer,
As will keep out the wind and the weather.

Christmas Morning

BY KATHARINE PYLE

St. Nicholas (December 1890)

On Christmas day, when fires were lit,
 And all our breakfasts done,
We spread our toys out on the floor
 And played there in the sun.

The nursery smelled of Christmas tree,
 And under where it stood
The shepherds watched their flocks of sheep,
 —All made of painted wood.

Outside the house the air was cold
 And quiet all about,
Till far across the snowy roofs
 The Christmas bells rang out.

But soon the sleigh-bells jingled by
 Upon the street below,
And people on the way to church,
 Went crunching through the snow.

We did not quarrel once all day;
 Mama and Grandma said
They liked to be in where we were,
 So pleasantly we played.

I do not see how any child
 Is cross on Christmas day,
When all the lovely toys are new,
 And everyone can play.

Church in City at Christmastime, 1945

Is It My Turn Yet?, 1946

I Saw Mommy Kissing Santa Claus

BY THOMAS CONNOR

I saw Mommy kissing Santa Claus
Underneath the mistletoe last night.
　　She didn't see me creep
　　Down the stairs to have a peep;
She thought that I was tucked up
　　In my bedroom fast asleep.

Then, I saw Mommy tickle Santa Claus
Underneath his beard so snowy white;
　　Oh, what a laugh it would have been
　　If Daddy had only seen
Mommy kissing Santa Claus last night.

Christmas Greeting

Sing hey! Sing hey!
For Christmas Day;
Twine mistletoe and holly,
For friendship glows
In winter snows,
And so let's all be jolly.

Hi! Ho! Santa, 1964

Santa's Perfect Form, 1981

At Christmas Play

BY THOMAS TUSSER

At Christmas play, and make
    good cheer,
For Christmas comes but once
    a year.

The Mistletoe

BY CLINTON SCOLLARD (c. 1870)

It was after the maze and mirth of the dance,
    Where a spray of green mistletoe swayed,
That I met—and I vow that the meeting was
        chance!—
    With a very adorable maid.

I stood for a moment in tremor of doubt,
    Then kissed her, half looking for war:
But—"Why did you wait, Sir!" she said, with a
        pout,
    "Pray, what is the mistletoe for?"

Mommy Kissing Santa Claus, circa 1953

ABOVE: *Santa's Little Buddy,* 1969

OPPOSITE: Vernon Grant with gnomes, circa 1940

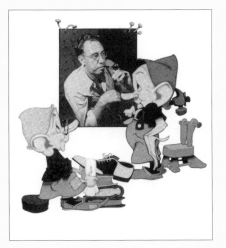

Afterword

One morning in 1910, on the plains of South Dakota, a spunky eight-year-old boy by the name of Vernon Grant declared, "When I grow up, I'm going to be an artist. I am going to draw pictures for kids, millions of kids." And that's exactly what he did.

As far back as he could remember, Vernon Grant aspired to be an artist. When he was four years old, his grandfather gave him a box of crayons and watercolors for his birthday. From that time on, it seemed that anyone who came with presents brought young Vernon art supplies. His mother saved wrappings from cracker boxes for Vernon to draw on, and at age ten he made himself a drawing table out of apple crates. Above the drawing table, he mounted shelves to store his pencils, watercolors, and crayons. The waist-high coulee that ran behind their homestead provided Vernon the

clay from which he modeled cowboys, Indians, horses, and the whimsical gnomes that later made him famous.

It soon became clear that this young lad had a very special gift: the talent to imagine and create. Beyond that, he had a "hankerin'" to succeed. Vernon drew inspiration from all of life's experiences, yet he was particularly fascinated with humor, make-believe, and small objects such as insects, frogs, and the tiny clay gnomes that he made. He listened intently to the fairy tales and stories told by his teacher in their one-room school. He journeyed far from home for private art lessons, and years later worked odd jobs to pay for his classes at the Chicago Art Institute. He was determined to lay the foundations that would help him succeed in the competitive world of commercial art.

During the difficult and trying times of the Great Depression and World War II, American industries looked for upbeat ways to promote their products. Vernon Grant's light, original approach to art was exactly what advertisers, publishers, and companies such as Hershey's, Gillette,

General Electric, and Oscar Mayer were seeking. Grant's humorous illustrations brought levity and reassurance to people during all the hardship, turmoil, and rapid changes that occurred. He held up a friendly mirror to the troubled society in which he lived.

Grant's style was unmistakably his own. A revered member of the Society of Illustrators in New York, Grant felt that fantasy is not something learned in art school. "It must be developed by the individual through his own personal imaginative powers," he often stated. Vernon Grant's career spanned seven decades, producing thousands of his distinctive gnomes, caricatures, and nursery rhyme illustrations. His greatest claim to fame was the creation of *Snap!*® *Crackle!*® *Pop!*® for the Kellogg Company. His images sold a multitude of products including cereal, batteries, chocolates, playing cards, and magazines. Appealing to both children and adults, Grant's characters expressed a feeling of warmth and humor. His use of vivid color and his genius for crisp, imaginative characterizations influenced illustrators and animators around the world, including Walt Disney.

That ambitious little boy's prediction long ago on the plains of South Dakota definitely came true. Vernon Grant became a successful artist and drew pictures for millions of kids—and adults—who will continue to see them and smile for generations to come. His is a lasting gift.

—MLN

OPPOSITE: Image from Vernon Grant's business card, circa 1929

ACKNOWLEDGMENTS

Santa Claus and Vernon Grant . . . together they have delighted millions of kids of all ages over the past century. Santa, the legendary toy maker with a heart of gold, and Vernon, the whimsical illustrator with the golden touch, are the stars of this timeless holiday collection. This latest offering gathers memorable literary excerpts spanning two centuries and reunites the successful team of Harry N. Abrams, Inc. and the Museum of York County. This same duo combined their talents to publish Grant's popular Mother Goose book in 1998. This book is dedicated to Vernon's late widow Lib and his children Kay and Chip for their willingness to share this dynamic collection of art with future generations. Mr. Claus and Mr. Grant had a stellar cast that worked behind the scenes to make this project possible. We acknowledge the leadership and vision of the York County Culture and Heritage Commission and the Vernon Grant Advisory Committee. And special thanks is extended to the Museum's Curator of Art Mary Lynn Norton, Museum store manager Bobbie Roberts, and CHC Executive Director Van Shields for their passion and dedication to the Vernon Grant legacy. May the Christmas spirit endure forever in popular culture through the legacies of Santa and Vernon Grant!

Allan M. Miller
York County Culture & Heritage Commissioner

TITLE PAGE: *Santa Checking It Twice,* 1977

Designer: Angela Carlino

Library of Congress Cataloging-in-Publication Data

Grant, Vernon, 1902-1990
Vernon Grant's Santa Claus / Mary Lynn Norton; illustrations by
Vernon Grant; accompanied by traditional Christmas readings.
    p. cm.
Summary: A collection of Christmas poetry and writings accompanied by
illustrator Vernon Grant's (1902-1990) paintings.
ISBN 0-8109-4518-5
1. Santa Claus—Literary collections. 2. Children's literature. [1.
Santa Claus—Literary collections.] I. Title: Santa Claus. II. Norton,
Mary Lynn. III. Title.

 PZ5.G6957Ve 2003
 [Fic]—dc21

                        2003001443

Printed and bound in Hong Kong
10 9 8 7 6 5 4 3 2 1

Harry N. Abrams, Inc.
100 Fifth Avenue
New York, N.Y. 10011
www.abramsbooks.com

Abrams is a subsidiary of

Giddy Up! It's Christmas!, 1955